Dedicated to Fred and Alice Tibbetts.
– Adam

Copyright © 2021 Clavis Publishing Inc., New York

Visit us on the Web at www.clavis-publishing.com.

Go Out and Play written by Adam Ciccio and illustrated by Katrien Benaets

ISBN 978-1-60537-646-2

This book was printed in August 2021 at Nikara, M. R. Štefánika 858/25, 963 01 Krupina, Slovakia.

First Edition
10 9 8 7 6 5 4 3 2 1

Clavis Publishing supports the First Amendment and celebrates the right to read.

Written by Adam Ciccio
Illustrated by Katrien Benaets

Go Out And Play

Clavis

NEW YORK

The clouds are gone and
the sun's face has shown.
It's time to walk away
from the tablet, TV, and phone.

We only have a handful of hours
before the sunshine gets low.
Let's move! Let's live! Let's go!

Grab a skateboard and
learn some *new tricks*.

Make a fort in the woods
out of fallen trees and broken sticks.

What if we pretend to be explorers
and go for a beautiful hike?
How do you know what you'll love
until you go out and see what you like?

Let's find some *new bugs* hiding under a rock.

Maybe try some *cannon balls*
off of an old dock.

Bring Grandpa on his boat for some *fishing.*

Throw some coins down a water well and *start wishing*.

Skip a flat rock on a glassy lake.

Memories are made
by the experiences you make.

Dust off that soccer ball
and *call a friend*.

Explore a field
that doesn't have an end.

Go get busy before that sun starts to fade.
There are trees that are missing you
under their shade.

Let's look through *a telescope*
and explore a new planet or star.

Help your dad build *the fastest man-made soapbox car*.

When the day is done and you
want to *rest your sleepy head,*
you can pick up this book
and drift off to bed.

You'll dream of the things
that you did with your day.
And tomorrow you'll get back out there.
You'll go out and play.